BISON
BOOKS

D0830553

Books by Mari Sandoz published by
the University of Nebraska Press

The Battle of the Little Bighorn
The Beaver Men: Spearheads of Empire
The Buffalo Hunters: The Story of the Hide Men
Capital City
The Cattlemen: From the Rio Grande across the Far Marias
Cheyenne Autumn
The Christmas of the Phonograph Records
Crazy Horse: The Strange Man of the Oglalas
The Horsecatcher
Hostiles and Friendlies: Selected Short Writings of Mari Sandoz
Letters of Mari Sandoz
Love Song to the Plains
Miss Morissa: Doctor of the Gold Trail
Old Jules
Old Jules Country
Sandhill Sundays and Other Recollections
Slogum House
Son of the Gamblin' Man: The Youth of an Artist
The Story Catcher
These Were the Sioux
The Tom-Walker
Winter Thunder

Mari Sandoz:

WINTER
THUNDER

University of Nebraska Press
Lincoln and London

First Bison Book Printing: 1986

Library of Congress Cataloging-in-Publication Data
Sandoz, Mari, 1896–1966.
   Winter thunder.
   Previously published as: The lost school bus. 1951.
   "Bison."
   Summary: When a school bus overturns in a blinding
blizzard, a young teacher and her pupils are stranded
miles from anywhere for eight days.
   [1. Survival—Fiction.   2. Blizzards—Fiction]
I. Title.
PS3537.A667L67   1986   [Fic]   85-20977
ISBN 0-8032-4167-4
ISBN 0-8032-9161-2 (pbk.)

Reprinted by arrangement with The Westminster Press.

♾

To MY NIECE CELIA,

daughter of Young Jules Sandoz, who, with her pupils, was lost and found in the blizzard of 1949

WINTER THUNDER

THE SNOW began quietly this time, like an afterthought to the gray Sunday night. The moon almost broke through once, but toward daylight a little wind came up and started white curls, thin and lonesome, running over the old drifts left from the New Year storm. Gradually the snow thickened, until around eight thirty the two ruts of the winding trails were covered and undisturbed except down in the Lone Tree district, where an old yellow bus crawled heavily along, feeling out the ruts between the choppy sand hills.

As the wind rose the snow whipped against the posts of a ranch fence across the trail, and caked against the bus windows, shutting in the young faces pressed to the glass. The storm increased until all the air was a powdery white and every hill, every trace of road, was obliterated. The bus wavered and swayed in its direction, the tracks filling in close upon the wheels as they sought out the trail lost somewhere far back, and then finally grasped at any footing, until it looked like some great snowy, bewildered bug seen momentarily through the shifting wind. But it kept moving, hesitating here, stalling there in the deepening drifts, bucking heavily into them, drawing back to try once more while the chains spun out white fans that were lost in the driving snow which seemed almost as thick, as dense. Once the bus had to back down from a steep little patch that might have led into a storm-lost valley with a ranch house and warmth and shelter. It started doggedly around, slower now, but decisive, feeling cautiously for traction on the drifted hillside. Then the wheels began to slip, catch, and then slip again, the bus tipping precariously in the push of the wind, a cry inside lost under the rising noise of the storm.

For a long time it seemed that the creeping bus could not be stopped. Even when all discernible direction or purpose was finally gone, it still moved, backing, starting again, this way and that, plowing the deepened slope, swaying, leaning until it seemed momentarily very tall and held from toppling only by the thickness of the flying snow. Once more a wheel caught and held under the thunder of the red-hot smoking exhaust. It slipped, and held again, but now the force of the wind was too great. For a moment the tilting bus seemed to lift. Then it pivoted into a slow skid and turned half around, broadside. Slowly it went over, almost as though without weight at all, settling lightly against a drift, to become a part of it at that thickening place where the white storm turned to snowbanks, lost except that there were frightening cries from inside, and a hiss of steam and smoke from the hot engine against the snow.

In a moment the door was forced outward, the wind catching a puff of smoke as dark, muffled heads pushed up and were white in an instant. They were children, mostly in snowsuits and in sheepskin coats, thrust down over the bus side, coughing and gasping as the force of the blizzard struck them, the older ones hunching their shoulders to shield themselves and some of the rest.

Once more the engine roared out and the upper back wheel spun on its side, free and foolish in its awkward caking of snow. Then the young woman who had handed the children down followed them, her sheepskin collar up about her head, her arms full of blankets and lunch boxes.

"You'll have to give it up, Chuck," she called back into the smoking interior. "Quick! Bring the rest of the lunches —"

With Chuck, sixteen and almost as tall as a man, beside her, Lecia Terry pushed the frightened huddle of children together and hurried them away downwind into the wall of storm. Once she tried to look back through the smother of snow, wishing that they might have taken the rope and shovel from the toolbox. But there was no time to dig for them on the under side now.

Back at the bus thick smoke was sliding out the door into the snow that swept along the side. Flames began to lick up under the leaning windows, the caking of ice suddenly running from them. The glass held one moment and burst, and the flames whipped out, torn away by the storm as the whole bus was suddenly a wet, shining yellow that blistered and browned with the heat. Then there was a dull explosion above the roar of the wind, and down the slope the fleeing little group heard it and thought they saw a dark fragment fly past overhead.

"Well, I guess that was the gas tank going," Chuck shouted as he tried to peer back under his shielding cap. But there was only the blizzard closed in around them, and the instinctive fear that these swift storms brought to all living creatures, particularly the young.

There was sobbing among the children now, a small one crying out, "Teacher! Teacher!" inside the thick scarf about her face, clutching for Lecia in her sudden panic.

"Sh-h, Joanie. I'm right here," the young woman soothed, drawing the six-year-old to her, looking around for the others, already so white that she could scarcely see them in the powdery storm.

"Bill, will you help Chuck pack all the lunches in two, three boxes, tight, so nothing gets lost? Maggie's big sirup bucket'll hold a lot. Throw all the empties away.

We'll have to travel light — " she said, trying to make it sound a little like an old joke.

"My father will be coming for me soon — " the eight-year-old Olive said primly. "So you need not touch my lunch."

"Nobody can find us here," Chuck said shortly, and the girl did not reply, too polite to argue. But now one of the small boys began to cry. "I want my own lunch box too, Teacher," he protested, breathless from the wind. "I — I want to go home!"

His older brother slapped him across the ear muffs with a mittened hand. "Shut up, Fritz," he commanded. "You can't go home. The bus is — " Then he stopped, looking toward the teacher, almost lost only an arm's length away, and the full realization of their plight struck him. "We can't go home," he said, so quietly that he could scarcely be heard in the wind. "The bus is burned and Chuck and Miss Lecia don't know where we are — "

"Sure we know!" Chuck shouted against him without looking up from the lunch packing, his long back stooped protectively over his task. "Don't we know, Lecia? Anyway, it won't last. Radio this morning said just light snow flurries, or Dad wouldn't have let me take the bus out 'stead of him, even sick as he was." The tall boy straightened up, the lunch boxes strung to the belt of his sheepskin to bang together in the wind until they were snow-crusted. " Baldy Stever'll be out with his plane looking for his girl friend soon's it clears a little, won't he, Lecia? " he said. " Like he came New Year's, with skis on it."

But the bold talk did not quiet the sobbing, and the teacher's nod was lost in the storm as she tied scarves and mufflers across the faces of the younger children, leaving only little slits for the eyes, with the brows and lashes already furred with snow. Then she lined up the seven, mixing the ages from six-year-old Joanie to twelve-year-old Bill, who limped heavily as he moved in the deepening snow. One of the blankets she pinned around the thinly dressed Maggie, who had only a short out-grown coat, cotton stockings, and torn overshoes against the January storm. The other blanket she tied around herself, ready to carry Joanie on her back, Indian fashion, when the short little legs were worn out.

Awkwardly, one after another, Lecia pulled the left arm of each pupil from the sleeve, buttoned it inside the coat and then tied the empty sleeve to the right arm of the one ahead. She took the lead, with little Joanie tied to her belt, where she could be helped. Chuck was at the tail end of the clumsy little queue, just behind Bill with the steel-braced ankle.

" Never risk getting separated," Lecia remembered hearing her pioneer grandfather say when he told of bury-ing the dead from the January blizzard of 1888 here, the one still called the school children's storm. "Never get separated and never stop moving until you find shelter — "

The teacher squinted back along the line, moving like some long snowy winter-logged animal, the segmented back bowed before the sharpening blizzard wind. Just the momentary turn into the storm took her breath and frightened her for these children hunched into themselves, half of them crying softly, hopelessly, as though already lost. They must hurry. With not a rock anywhere and not a tree within miles to show the directions, they had to seek out the landmark of the ranch country — the wire fence. So the girl started downwind again, breaking the new drifts as she searched for valley ground where fences were most likely, barbed-wire fences that might lead to a ranch, or nowhere except around some hay meadow. But it was their only chance the girl from the sand hills knew. Stumbling, floundering through the snow, she kept the awkward string moving, the eyes of the older ones straining through frozen lashes for even the top of one fence post, those of the small ones turned in upon their fear as the snow caked on the mufflers over their faces and they stumbled blindly to the pull from ahead.

Once there was a bolt of lightning, milky white in the blizzard, and a shaking of thunder, ominous winter thunder that stopped the moving feet. Almost at once the wind grew sharper, penetrating even Chuck's heavy sheepskin coat, numbing the ears and feet as panting, sobbing, the children plowed on again, the new drifts soon far above Lecia's boots, and no visibility, no way to avoid them.

With their hands so awkwardly useless, someone stumbled every few steps, but the first to fall was the crippled Bill, the others, the crying ones too, standing silent in the storm, not even able to slap one frozen hand against another while the boy was helped up. After that others went down, and soon it was all that the teacher and the boy Chuck could do to keep the children moving as they pushed through the chop hills and found themselves going up what seemed a long wind-swept, wind-frozen slope, Lecia carrying Joanie on her back most of the time now. But they kept moving somehow, barely noticing even the jack rabbit that burst out among their feet and was gone into the storm. Otherwise there was nothing.

After a long, long time they reached what seemed a high ridge of hills standing across the full blast of the north wind that bent them low and blinded. Suddenly Chuck's feet slid off sideways into a hole, a deep-cupped blowout hidden by the storm. Before he could stop, he had drawn the rest tumbling in after him, with an avalanche of snow. Crying, frightened, the smaller ones were set to their feet and brushed off a little. Then they all crouched together under the bank to catch their breath out of the wind, shivering, wet from the snow that had fallen inside their clothes, which were already freezing hard as board.

"With the blowouts always from the northwest to the southeast," Chuck shouted into the teacher's covered ear, "the wind's plainly from the north, so we're being pushed about due south. That direction there can't be a house for five, six miles, even if we could find it — unless we got clear out of our home country — "

The girl shivered, empty with fear. " — So that's why we haven't found a fence," she said slowly. "We're probably in the old Bar M summer range, miles and miles across. But we can't go any other direction — "

"I could alone; I could make it out alone!" Chuck shouted suddenly, angrily.

For a moment the teacher was silent, waiting, but when he added nothing more, she said: "You can't leave these little ones now, Chuck. Even if you were sure you could find a ranch — "

There was no reply, except that the crippled boy began to cry, a reddening from his ankle coming up through the snow that was packed into his overshoes around the brace. Others were sobbing too, and shaking with cold, but the younger ones were very quiet now, already drowsing, and so the young teacher had to get to her feet and help lift the children out of the blowout. Slapping the muffler-covered cheeks, shaking the smaller ones so hard that the caked snow fell from them, she got the line moving again, but very slowly. She was worn out too, from the path-breaking and with Joanie in her arms to warm the child, keep her from the sleep of freezing that came upon her on Lecia's back, with only the thin blanket against the ice of the wind.

They seemed to be going down now, through a long deep-drifted slope, plowing into buried yucca clumps, the sharp spears penetrating the snowsuits, even the boot tops. Here a few head of cattle passed them, less than three feet away and barely to be seen. They were running, snow-caked, blinded, bawling, and Lecia squinted anxiously back into the storm for others, for a herd that might be upon them, trample them as surely as stampeding buffaloes. But there were no more now, and she could see that Chuck was shouting, " Little chance of its clearing up soon, with that snow thunder and those cattle already drifting so fast — all the way from the winter range! "

Yes, drifting fast with the force and terror of the storm, even hardy, thick-haired range cattle running!

Then suddenly one of the younger boys cried out something. " Teacher! " he repeated, " I saw a post! "

But it must have been a trick of the wind, for there was only the driving snow, except that the sharp-eyed Maggie saw one too, ahead and to the right — a snowy post with only the upper foot or so out of the drifts, holding up a strand of gray wire taut and humming in the cold.

For a moment Lecia could not see through the blurring of her eyes. At least this was something to follow, but which way? To her signal Chuck lifted his arm and dropped it. He didn't recognize the fence either, and so the teacher took the easier direction, leftward, only sideface to the wind, although it might lead to the hills, to some final drift as the fleeing cattle would end.

Moving slowly along the fence, Lecia knew that it could not be much farther anyway. Her arms were wooden with cold and the weight of the child, her legs so weary in the deepening drifts that with each step it seemed that she could never lift a snow-caked boot again.

Then suddenly Chuck was doubling up the line. " I think I know where we are! That old split post just back there's where we made a take-down running coyotes with Dad's hounds this fall. If I'm right, this is Miller's north meadow, and there's a strip of willows down ahead there, off to the right — "

For a moment the girl set Joanie into the deep snow, panting, and even when she caught her breath, she was afraid to speak.

" How far to a house? " she finally asked, her lips frozen.

" There's no house along this fence if it's the Miller, "

Chuck had to admit. " It just goes around the meadow, three, four miles long."

" You're sure — " the teacher asked slowly, " — sure there's no cross fence to the ranch? You might get through, find help in time — "

The boy could only shake his snowy head and then, thinking that the storm hid this, he shouted the words on the wind. No, no cross fence, and the ranch was five miles south. Not even a haystack left in the valley here. Miller had had his hay balers in this fall, hauled it all out for his fancy Angus herd.

Then they must take a chance on the willows, with Bill hardly able to limp along, Joanie too heavy to carry, and several others worn out. So they wallowed through the drifted fence and tried to keep parallel to its direction, but far enough in the meadow to see any willows. There must be willows now.

Suddenly Lecia went down in what must have been a deep gully, the ground gone, the girl sinking into soft powdery snow to her shoulder. Panting, choking, she managed to get Joanie and the rest back out and the frightened ones quieted a little. Then she swung off right along the barer edge of the gully, seeking a place to cross. The wind was blowing in powerful gusts now, so that she could scarcely stand up. Bent low she dragged at the line behind her, most of the children crawling in the trench she plowed for them. There was no crying now

— only the slow, slow moving. Perhaps they should dig into the snow here below the gully bank. Indians and trappers had done that and survived. But they had thick-furred buffalo robes to shut out the cold and snow, and they were grown men, tough, strong — not helpless, worn-out children, their frozen feet heavy as stone, with only an overgrown boy and a twenty-three-year-old girl to lead them, keep them alive.

More and more often Lecia had to stop, her head down, her arms dropping the weight of the little girl. But there seemed to be a shallowing in the gully now, and so it was time she tried to break a path through it and turned back toward the fence if they were not to wander lost as so many did that other time, long ago, when a teacher and her nine pupils were lost, finally falling to die on the prairie. They must cling to the fence here, if it went no farther than around the meadow. At least it was proof that something existed on the earth except the thick, stinging blizzard, with a white, freezing, plodding little queue caught in the heart of it, surrounded.

Once when the girl looked up from the running snow it seemed there was something darkish off to the right, little farther than arm's reach away. She saw it again, something rounded, perhaps a willow clump, low, snow filled, and possibly with more near by. Signaling to Chuck, Lecia turned down to it — a willow covered as in sleep, but with at least two more bushes just beyond, larger, darker, and standing closer together, their longer upper arms snow-weighted, entwined over the drifts. There, between the clumps, out of the worst of the storm, she left the children squatted close, the blankets held over them. With the belts of her coat and Chuck's, they tied the longer brushy tops of the two clumps together as solidly as they could. Then, fighting the grasping wind, they managed to fasten the blankets across the gap between the willows, to hold awhile. Behind this protection Lecia dug through the snow to the frozen ground while Chuck gathered dead wood. Inside a close little kneeling circle of children they built a fire pile with some dry inner bark and a piece of sandwich paper for the lighting. Awkwardly, with freezing hands the teacher and Chuck hurried, neither daring to think about matches, dry ones, in any pocket after this stumbling and falling through the snow.

The two smaller children were dropping into the heavy sleep of exhaustion and cold and had to be held in their places by the older ones while Chuck dug swiftly through his pockets, deeper, more awkwardly, then frantically, the circle of peering eyes like those of fearful young animals, cornered, winter-trapped.

Down to his shirt, Chuck found some in his pocket, six in a holder made of two rifle cartridges slipped together. Hurrying clumsily he struck one of the matches. It sputtered and went out, the flames sucked away. They had to try again, making a closer circle, with the coat-tails of the children thrown up over their heads to shut out the storm. This time the match caught on the waxed paper and the diamond willow began to snap and sizzle in the snow, throwing a dancing light up to the circle of crouching children.

But it seemed even colder now that they had stopped walking and Lecia thought of the night ahead, with the temperature surely down to twenty-five or thirty below zero. Beyond that she would not look now; but to get through this night they must have a great pile of wood, and they must have shelter even to hold the fire.

" We can't both go out at one time," the teacher told Chuck in their planning, somehow making it seem as for a long, long time. " It's too risky for the children. We might not get back."

The boy looked around from the fire he was nursing, and upward, but there was still no thinning of the storm, the area of snowy visibility almost as small as the con-fines of their new meat-freeze room at the ranch. Even so he gave the girl no sign of agreement.

Lecia set willow poles into the snowbanks as she went to look for wood, none farther apart than the outstretched reach of her arms. She found more willows, each clump sitting alone in the isolation of the driving storm, so cold now that the green wood snapped off like glass. Each time it was only by the row of sticks in the drifts that she managed to stagger her blinded and panting way back against the wind with her load of wood.

The brushier portions she piled behind the blankets of the shelter to catch the snow and shut out the wind. Some, long as fish poles, she pushed through the willow clumps and across the opening between, in a sort of lattice inside the bellying blankets that Eddie and Calla tried to hold in place. They were the first of the children to separate themselves from the snowy composite, the enforced co-ordinate that had been the queue driven by the storm, the circle that shielded the sprouting fire. Now they were once more individuals who could move alone, hold the blankets from blowing inward, pile the dry powdery snow from the ground against and between the sticks, trying to work it like plaster, building a wall between the clumps of willows. Even Bill helped a little, as far as he could reach without moving the bad ankle. They worked slowly, clumsily, pounding their freezing hands at the fire, but returning.

By one o'clock the north wind was cut off so that the fire fattened and burned higher, softening the ice caked to the clothing until it could be knocked off, and softening the face of the drift reached by the wind-blown heat. The children packed this against the north wall too, and into the willow clumps both ways, drawing the rounded wall inward toward the top along the bend of the willows, making what looked like half of an Indian snow shelter, or the wickiup Calla had seen at the county fair, just high enough at the center for a seven-year-old to stand up, the snow walls glistening rosy in the firelight as the wind was shut off.

" That's a good job! " Chuck shouted over the roar of the storm as he tried to rub circulation into Joanie's waxen feet. The small girl was beginning to cry out of her sleep with the first pain; others began too, their ears and hands swollen and purpling, their toes painful as their boots thawed. But it seemed that the feet of nine-year-old Maggie must be lost, the ragged old overshoes and cotton stockings so frozen that she had to cut them away with Eddie's knife. Under them her feet were like stone, dead white stone, although the girl was working hard to rub life into them. She worked silently and alone, as had become natural long ago, her thin face pinched and anxious with the pain and the alarm.

Of them all only Olive seemed untouched. She was dry in her heavy waterproofed snowsuit with attached rubber feet inside the snow boots. And she was still certain that her father would soon come for her.

" He would not care to leave me in such an unpleasant place — "

When they had the semicircular wall of the shelter drawn in as far as the snow would hold, Lecia decided to pull the blankets away from the outside and use one over the top, with the belt-tied willows sticking through a

smoke hole cut in the center. But as the blankets came
down, part of the loose snow wall was blown in by the
force of the blizzard, the huddle of children suddenly
white again, the fire almost smothered. So the wall had
to be rebuilt in discouragement, but with care, using
more brush and sticks, more fire-softened snow to freeze
in place as soon as it was struck by the storm. Lecia had
to stop several times for her hands too, pounding them
hard, holding them over the fire, the diamond sparkling.
She tried to turn the ring off before the swelling became
too great and then gave it up. The wall must be finished,
and when it was solid, Calla came to whisper under the
roar of the wind. " Bill's been eating the lunch," she said.

" Oh, Bill! That's not fair to the others, to your own
little sister Joanie! " Lecia cried. Suddenly not the good
teacher, she grabbed up the containers and hung them
on high branches out in plain sight for watching, for re-
minders and derision from the other children. " Why, it
may be days before we are found! " she scolded, in her
exasperation saying what should have been kept hidden
in silence.

Before the boy could defend himself with a plea of
hunger or his usual complaint about the crippled foot,
some realization of their plight had struck the others.
Even little Fritz, with the security of an older sister and
brother like Calla and Eddie along, began to sob. Only
the round-cheeked Olive was calm, the others angered to

see it, wanting to shout against her outsider's assurance, to tell her she was too stupid and green to know that her father could not come for her in such a blizzard, that he would never find her if he could get through. But they were silent under the teacher's admonitory eye. And, as in the schoolhouse and on the playground, Bill had withdrawn, except that now it could not be more than a foot or two.

As the frozen earth between the willow humps became soggy, Calla and Eddie helped move the others around so that there was room to draw the fire first one way and then another, to dry and warm the ground. Lecia watched to see that they set no one afire and then bowed her head out into the storm again. Chuck was dragging in willows for the night. They drove sticks into the hardening drifts around the front of the shelter and piled brush against them to catch the snow. It filled in as fast as they worked until there was no more than a little crawling hole left. Then Chuck laid a mat of brushy sticks on the ground and packed soft snow into them to freeze, making a handled slab big enough to close the low doorway. Now, so long as the blanket with the smoke hole stayed tied over the top they could be as warm as they wished in the little shelter that was scarcely longer than a tall man — a close cramping for the teacher, Chuck, and the seven pupils, but easily warmed with a few fingers of wood, an Indian fire. Safe and warm so long as the shelter stood against the rising ferocity of the blizzard, and the willows lasted.

By now the cold stung the nose and burned the lungs, the snow turned to sharp crystals that drew blood from the bare skin. It drove the teacher and Chuck in to the fire, shaking, unable, it seemed, ever to be warmed through again. Lecia opened her sheepskin coat, hung up her frozen scarf and cap and shook out her thick brown hair that gleamed in the firelight. Even with her tawny skin red and swollen, her gold-flecked hazel eyes bloodshot, she was still a pretty girl, and the diamond on her hand flashed as she hunted for her stick of white salve to pass around for the raw, bleeding lips. It was all she could do.

Now they tried to plan for what was to come, but here they were as blind as in the flight through the storm. There would be sickness, with the noses already running, Joanie coughing deep from her chest, and, worst of all, Maggie's feet that seemed to be dying. Besides, the fire must be kept going and the food spread over three, perhaps four, days.

Here Bill raised his complaining voice. "You ain't our boss outside of school! We'll do what we want to. There ain't enough to eat for everybody."

"You mean *isn't,* not *ain't,*" the teacher corrected firmly. "And talking like that — when you've barely missed one lunch time!"

"You ain't never my boss," Chuck said casually, " — only about the kids while in the bus, like you do with my dad when he's driving. I sure can do what I want to here, and I'll do it."

Slowly the girl looked around the ring of drowsy, firelit eyes upon her, some uneasy at this bold talk to their teacher, but some smaller ones aping the defiance of the big boys. Chuck, who sat almost a head taller than Lecia, grinned down at the pretty young teacher but with an arrogance that was intended to remind her he saw nothing here as his responsibility, nothing this side of the bus except saving himself.

Unable to reply in words that would not frighten the children more, the teacher looked past the fire into the boy's broad, defiant face, into his unblinking, storm-red eyes, the look commanding at first, then changing to something else in spite of herself, into a sort of public test, until it seemed she dared not turn her gaze away or at that instant the sixteen-year-old boy must assert his victory by plunging out into the storm and perhaps destroy himself, perhaps bring death to all of them.

Before this silent, incomprehensible struggle the children were uneasy and afraid, even the coughing stilled, so that the storm seemed very loud outside the smoke hole. But little Fritz was too young to be held so for long. "I'm hungry!" he shouted against the restraining hand of his sister. "I want my lunch!"

As though freed, released, Chuck sat back and grinned a little at the small boy. Matter of factly the teacher washed her raw hands with snow and held them over the fire. Then she spread her napkin on her lap and set out all there was in the eight lunches now: fourteen sandwiches, most of them large, six pieces of Sunday cake, a handful of cookies, a few pieces of candy, and six apples and two oranges, frozen hard. There were two thermos bottles of milk, and these Lecia pushed away into the snow wall.

"If somebody gets sick and can't eat solid food," she said to the owners, their eyes following her hands in consternation. Even with the best management, there would be no food of any kind in a few days, but this the small owners could not yet understand.

The frozen fruit she handed to Chuck and, without meeting the girl's eyes, he set it around the coals for toasting, to be eaten now because it would not keep well, and might sicken leaner stomachs. In the meantime Lecia set one lunch box filled with snow near the fire and packed away all except four of the big sandwiches into the others, the eyes of the children following her hands here too, even as she hung the containers back above her head. Then she divided the four sandwiches into halves and passed them around.

"Eat very slowly," she cautioned. "Blizzards usually

last three days, so we must make what we have here last too, probably clear to Thursday, or longer."

But Bill seemed not to be listening. "Chuck's eating!" he suddenly protested. "He ain't, *isn't,* in on the lunches."

For a moment the teacher looked sternly at the boy. "After Chuck carried them all from the bus, helped you through the bad places, and helped to make the shelter and the fire!" the girl said in astonishment. "Now we'll have no more of this bickering and complaint. Here we are equal partners, and not one of us will get out of this alive unless we keep working together. Even your comic books should have taught you that much! And don't think this is play. You remember what the storm of 1888 was called in your history book — because so many school children died in it. That storm was short, not over two days most places, nothing for length like the one we had holiday time this year, and no telling about this one. Most of the children in 1888 died because somebody got panicky, didn't think, or they didn't stick together — "

There was silence all around the fire now, the storm seeming to rise, the children edging closer to each other, glancing fearfully over their shoulders as though toward night windows with terrible things stalking outside.

"Oh, we're O.K.," Chuck said optimistically. "We can

last three days easy here — " the rebellion gone from him, or hidden for the moment.

Thinking of a five-day storm, the teacher looked around the frightened, sooty faces, the children coughing and sniffling, their pocket tissue gone, the few handkerchiefs hung to dry and wondered if any, even the man-tall Chuck, would be here by then.

But Olive, the newcomer, was unconcerned. "I should like another sandwich, Miss Terry. From my own lunch, please," she said, with the formality of an old-fashioned boarding school for eight-year-olds. "I won't need the remainder. My father will come for me when it is time."

"He won't find you — " Maggie said as she rubbed at her feet, color seeping into them now, an angry gray-splotched purple, with pain that twisted the thin face.

"My father will come," Olive repeated, plainly meaning that he was not like the fathers of the others here, particularly Maggie's, who had done nothing since the war except make a little South Pacific bug juice, as he called it, for himself from chokecherries, wild grapes, or raisins in the way they did in the war. He had only a little piece of copper tubing, and so he couldn't make more than enough for himself, yet he got into jail just the same, for crashing his old truck through the window of the county assistance office. But things had not been good before that. Often this fall Maggie was at school when the bus arrived, not waiting at the stop near their crumbling old sod shack but walking the three miles. Sometimes her face was bruised, but she was silent to any questioning. If Maggie lost her feet now, it was because she had no warm snowsuit and high boots like the others, only the short old coat above her skinny knees, the broken overshoes with the soles flopping.

But there was still a cheerful face at the fire. Although little Fritz's cheeks seemed swollen to bursting and his frosted ears stood away under the flaps of his cap, he could still show his gap-toothed grin in mischief.

"If we don't get home till Thursday, Teacher, Baldy'll be awful mad at you when he comes flying out Wednesday — "

The rest laughed a little, drowsily. "Maybe Baldy won't be flying around that soon," Eddie said, and was corrected by Calla's sisterly concern. "Don't say Baldy. Say Mr. Stever."

But the teacher busied herself hanging up everything loose. Then with Chuck's knife she slit the remaining blanket down the middle and fastened half around each side against the snow wall, like a tipi lining. By the time the white blizzard darkness came, the smaller children had all been taken outside for the last time and lay in fretful, uneasy sleep. Olive had been the last, waiting stubbornly for her father until she toppled forward. Calla caught her and made room for the girl still murmuring, "Papa — "

Finally the last sob for parent and home was stilled, even Joanie asleep, her feverish head in the teacher's lap, her throat raw and swelling, with nothing except hot snow water to ease the hollow cough. There were half a dozen lozenges in Lecia's pocket but these must be saved for the worse time that would surely come.

The children were packed around the fire like little pigs or puppies on a very cold night. Chuck was at the opposite side from Lecia, the boys on his side, the girls on hers, with Calla and her brothers around the back. The older ones lay nearer the wall, their arms over the younger to hold their restlessness from the fire.

But Bill was still up, drawn back under the willows, his heap pulled into his sheepskin collar, his ankle bent to him. He watched the teacher doze in fatigue, met her guilty waking gaze sullenly. But finally he reached down into his pocket and drew out something in waxed paper.

"I didn't eat the piece you gave me—" he said, holding out his half of the sandwich.

"Bill! That was fine of you," the girl said, too worn out for more as she reached up to put it away.

"No—no, you eat it. I guess you didn't take any."

A moment Lecia looked at the boy, but he avoided her as he edged himself around Chuck closer to the fire, turning his chilled back to the coals, and so she ate the buttered bread with the thick slice of strengthening cold beef, while more snow was driven in through the smoke hole and settled in sparkling dust toward the little fire. There were white flashes too, and the far rumble of winter thunder.

"Is — is there lots of willows left?" the crippled boy asked.

The teacher knew what he meant — how many clumps, and if so far out that someone might let lost.

"I think there are quite a few," she replied, needing to reassure the boy, but unable to make it a flat lie.

A long time he sat silent. Finally he pulled his cap off and shook the long yellowish hair back from his petulant face. "I wonder what Mother's doing —" he said slowly, looking away, his hand seeking out the tortured ankle. Lecia motioned him to hold it over to her and so she did not need to reply, to ask what all the mothers of these children must be doing, with the telephone lines still down from the other storm and surely nobody foolish enough to try bucking this one, unless it might be Olive's father, the new Eastern owner of the little Box Y ranch.

With snow water heated in the lunch tin, Lecia washed the poor stick that was the boy's ankle, gently sponging the bone laid almost bare where the frozen snow and the iron brace wore through the scarred and unhealthy skin.

"It looks pretty bad, Bill, but you probably won't have to put the brace back on for days —" Lecia started to comfort, but it was too late, and she had to see fear and anger and self-pity darken the face in the firelight. Because nothing could be unsaid, the girl silently bandaged the ankle with half of the boy's handkerchief. " Now get a little sleep if you can," she said gently.

The boy crawled in next to Eddie as though Ed were the older, and for a long time the teacher felt the dark eyes staring at her out of the shadowy coat collar as though she had deliberately maneuvered this plunge into the blizzard.

Several times before midnight the girl started to doze but jerked herself awake at the frozen creak of the willow shelter, to push the out-tossed arms back and replenish the fire.

Eddie's cough began to boom deep as from a barrel. He turned and moaned, digging at his chest, Calla helpless beside him, her sleep-weighted eyes anxious on the teacher. Maggie too was finally crying now. Her feet had puffed up and purpled dark as jelly bags, with the graying spots that would surely break and slough off, perhaps spread in gangrene. Yet all Lecia could do was turn the girl's feet from the fire and push them behind the blanket against the snow to relieve the pain and itching a little. Perhaps only freeze them more. Lecia touched the girl's forehead to calm her but felt her stiffen and start to pull away from this unaccustomed kindly touch. Then Maggie relaxed a little and as the teacher stroked the hot temples, she wondered how many days it might be before help could get through. Suddenly their plight here seemed so hopeless, the strength and wisdom of her twenty-three years so weak and futile, that she had to slip out into the storm for calm. And finally Maggie slept, worn out, but still tearing at her feet.

To the weary girl watching, half asleep, at the fire, the roar of the storm rose and fell like the panting of a great live thing, sometimes a little like many great planes warming up together. If only she had married Dale Stever New Year's, they would be in the Caribbean now, these children all safe at home, with probably no other teacher available so soon. Once Lecia turned her swollen hand to the fire, watching the ring catch and break the light into life, and tried to recall the fine plans Dale had made for them. He wasn't a rancher's son like those who usually took her to parties and dances — like Joe, or Wilmo, or even Ben, of the local bank. Dale had come from outside last summer and bought up the sale pavilion in town. Since then he flew all around the surrounding ranch country in a plane the color of a wild canary rising from a plum thicket, gathering stock for the sales. Fairtime he took Lecia and her friend Sallie down to the state fair, and several times on long trips since, to Omaha to the ballet and to Denver. At first it seemed he was all jolly big-talk, with windy stories of his stock in

an oil company down in Dallas and in a Chicago com-
mission house. He had a touch of gray at his temples that
he thought made him look distinguished when he had
his hat on, and to their fathers he called himself the
Dutch uncle of the two girls. But gradually he concen-
trated on Lecia, and at Christmas there was the big diamond and the plane ready to fly south. He even took her
to the school board to ask for a release from her contract.

" No," the old school director told the girl. " Bill Terry
was a friend of mine, brought me into the country. I
can't help his granddaughter marry no man in a rush
hurry."

Dale laughed confidently and put his arm about the
girl's shoulder as they left, but somehow Lecia couldn't
break her contract. They must wait until school was out.
Dale had been angry. " This is no life for a girl as pretty
as you," he said. Truly he was right. Today it was no
life for any girl.

Soon after midnight Lecia was startled out of a doze
by the sound of cattle bawling somewhere in the roar of
the storm, like the herds that passed her home in the
night of the May blizzard three years ago, when so many
died in the drifts and lakes that the whole region was a
stench far into the summer. Then suddenly the girl realized where she was, and hurried bareheaded out into the
storm. The bawling was very close; any moment hun-

dreds of storm-blinded cattle might be running over the little willows, over their own two clumps.

Lecia dragged burning sticks from the fire, but in an instant the storm had sucked their flame away. So, with her arms up to shield her eyes from the snow that was sharp as steel dust, she stood behind the shelter shouting the "Hi-ah! Hi-ah!" she had learned when she helped the cowboys push cattle to market. It was a futile, lost little sound against cattle compelled to run by an instinct that could not be denied, compelled to flee for survival before the descent of the arctic storm, never stopping until trapped in some drift, or boldly overtaken in some open fence corner to freeze on their feet, as Lecia had seen them stand.

Realizing her danger as a warmth crept over her, the girl stumbled back into the shelter and crouched at the fire. She barely noticed the sting of returning blood in her ears and face while she listened until the drifting herd was surely past, made more afraid by the knowledge of this thing that drove cattle galloping through the night, the power of it, and how easily it could overcome the little circle of children here if it were not for the handful of fire, for the walls of the storm's own snow.

Toward morning the weary girl knew that she could not keep awake. She had stirred Chuck to sit up a while, but he was unable to shake off the weight of sleep so heavy on an overgrown boy. Trying to remember how the Indians carried their fire — something about moss and damp, rotted wood — Lecia pulled old dead roots from the willow butts and laid them into the coals with the ends sticking far out. Even with waxed paper handy it would be a desperate chance. Willows burned fast as kindlings and there were only five matches, including the one from Eddie's pocket, and no telling how many spoiled by dampness.

Even so it was sweet to let herself sink into darkness, but it seemed that she awoke at once, stiff and cold from the nightmare that reached into the waking black, even the ashes of the fire spot cold. With the waxed paper held ready, the girl blew on the ends of the unburnt roots her hands found, carefully, breathless in her fear. At last a red spark glowed deep in one, and when the fire was going again, she slipped outside for calm in the cold that was like thin, sharp glass in the nose.

There was still no earth and no sky, only the white storm of late dawn blowing hard. But the wood had lasted and now Lecia put on a few extra sticks and heated water to wash the goose mush from the inflamed eyes of the children. She started a rousing song: "Get up! Get up, you sleepyhead!" but even before it was done, Joanie began to whimper, "I'm hungry—"

So the teacher laid out four sandwiches on sticks over the coals and then added another half for herself when she saw Bill watching. "There won't be anything more today except a pinch of cake unless the sun breaks through."

"If it does, we can stomp out a message on the snow," Calla said cheerfully.

"Yes, even if people can't travel for a whole week, Baldy'll come flying over to see about his girl friend," Bill said, boldly.

The younger boys laughed a little, but Chuck was more serious. "If the sky lightens at all and there's no blowing, I'll do the stomping before I leave."

"You'd run away now?" the teacher asked softly as she combed at Joanie's fine brown hair.

"Somebody's got to get help," he defended in loud words.

The children around the fire were suddenly quiet, turning their eyes to follow the tall boy as he pulled up his sheepskin collar and crawled out into the storm. And silent a long time afterward — all except Joanie, who sobbed softly, without understanding. Even Olive looked up once, but Maggie grated her feet hard along the snow wall and tore at their congestion as though she heard nothing.

Then suddenly there was stomping outside and Chuck came back in, snowy, thick frost all over his collar and cap, his brows and lashes in ice, the children pushing over toward him, as to one gone, lost. He brought more wood, and the teacher seemed to have forgotten that he had said anything about leaving. But the children watched him now, even when they pretended they didn't, and watched Lecia too, for suspicion had come in.

The teacher started as for a school day, except that the arithmetic was rote learning of addition and multiplication tables and a quick run through some trick problems: " If I had a fox, a goose, and some corn to get across a river in a boat — " and then, " If I had a dollar to buy a hundred eggs — no, I should take something that won't make us hungry."

" Like a hundred pencils? "

" Well, yes, let's take pencils. I want to buy a hundred for a dollar. Some are five cents each, poor ones two and a half cents, and broken ones half a cent. How many of each kind must I buy? "

In history and nature study they talked about the Indians that still roamed the sand hills when Lecia's grandfather came into the country. They lived the winter long in skin tipis something like the shelter here, and almost as crowded, but with piles of thick-furred buffalo robes for the ground and the beds. The girls sat on one side, the boys on the other.

" Like we are here — " Fritz said, his eyes shining in the discovery. " We're Indians. Whoo-oo-oo! " he cried, slapping his mouth with his palm.

They talked about the food too, the piles of dried and

pounded meat, the winter hunts, how the village and lodges were governed, and what the children did, their winter games, one almost like "button, button." The boys learned from the men — such things as arrow-making, and later bullet-making, hunting, fighting; and particularly the virtues of resourcefulness, courage, fortitude, and responsibility for all the people. A girl learned from the women — beading, tanning hides, and all the other things needed to live well with modesty, steadfastness, and generosity, and with courage and fortitude and responsibility too, for it was thought that the future of the people lay in the palms of the women, to be cherished or thrown away.

"What does that mean, Teacher?" Fritz asked, hitting out in mischief at his brother Eddie, despite Calla and the teacher both watching, then shouting he was hungry again.

The rest tried to laugh a little as Calla whispered to her small brother, trying to make herself heard against the storm, while Lecia taught them a poem about Indians. Even Joanie repeated a few lines for her, although the child leaned weak and feverish against Calla while Bill comforted his bound ankle and Maggie tried hard to pull herself out of the curious drowsiness that had the teacher frightened.

After a while the children played "button, button," and tried to tell each other poems. When Eddie got stuck on "Snowbound," Bill nudged Fritz and they laughed as easily at his discomfiture as at school, perhaps because Chuck was back and this was the second day of the storm, with tomorrow the third. Then it would clear up and somebody with a scoop shovel would get his horse along the barer ridges to a telephone.

"Maybe somebody'll just come running over the hills to find us," Eddie teased, looking at Olive, turning his face from the teacher.

Well, even if nobody came and Baldy couldn't find a place to land with skis on his plane, he would have sacks of food and blankets and stuff dropped like in the movies and the newspapers.

"I saw it in a movie once, I did," Joanie cried.

So they talked, pretending no one was looking up at the hanging lunch buckets, or sick and afraid. But Lecia did not hear them.

"Oh-oo, Teacher's sleeping like one of those old Indian women up to Gordon, just sitting there!" Eddie exclaimed.

"Sh-h," Calla said, in her way. "Let her stretch out here," and with a polite smile Olive moved aside.

That night Joanie was delirious, and once Maggie slipped past the teacher out into the storm to relieve the fire of her feet. By midnight she couldn't stand on them, and the grayish spots were yellow under the thick skin of a barefoot summer, the swelling creeping above the girl's thin ankles, with red streaks reaching almost to the knees. Her eyes glistened, her cheeks were burning, and she talked of wild and dreadful things.

Lecia tried to remember all that she had read of frostbite, all that her grandfather had told, but she knew that the inflammation spreading past the frozen area was like the cold overtaking the fleeing cattle, and she had to make a desperate decision. She dug two holes deep into the snow wall and laid Maggie with her feet in them almost to her knees, wishing they had something waterproof for covering. The cold would probably freeze the girl more, but it would numb the nerves and perhaps slow the congestion and tissue starvation. Later, when the girl was restless again and crying, Lecia found the yellow spots spreading, painful and hard as boils. She burned the end of a safety pin and while Maggie's frightened eyes became caverns in her thin face, Lecia opened one of the spots. Bloody pus burst down over her hand. Holding the foot aside she wiped it away on the snow, from her ring too, and then slipped it from her shrunken finger and hung it on a twig overhead, where it swayed a little, like a morning dewdrop while she opened the rest of the festering.

While the girl's feet were bathed and bound in the sleeves torn from Lecia's white shirt blouse, she thrust them back into the snow. Then she gave Maggie half a cup of the milk, very quietly, hoping none would awaken to see, although none needed it more. Almost at once the girl was asleep, to rest until the pus gathered again. But the first time Lecia returned with firewood she saw the thermos bottle half out. She jerked it from the hole. The milk was all gone, and across the little fire Olive stared at her teacher.

"It was mine," the girl said flatly.

So the time had come when the little food left must be hidden. Now, with all but Olive sleeping, was the time. When Lecia came back in, the girl held out some-thing — the ring that had been left hanging on the twig and forgotten.

The next day and the next were the same, only colder, the drifts deeper and harder along the willows, the wind so sharp with snow that it froze the eyeballs. Lecia and Chuck covered their faces as they fought their way back against it, the wood dragging from their shoulders, tied by a strap of cloth cut off around the bottom of Lecia's coat. One at a time they went out and came back, a hand stretched ahead feeling for the next guide pole in the snow before the other let go of the last, the covered face turned from the storm to save the breath from being torn away by the wind.

All the third day there was watching out of the smoke

hole for the sky that never appeared. When night finally came without star or stillness, even Lecia, who had tried to prepare herself for this eventuality, felt that she could not face another day of blizzard. Maggie no longer sat up now and both Joanie and Eddie were so sick — their fever high, their chests filling — that the teacher had to try something. She seemed to remember that the early settlers used willow bark to break a fever, so she steeped a handful in Maggie's tin cup until the liquid was strong and dark. She made the two children drink it, first experimentally, then more, and after a while they began to sweat. When they awoke they were wet, their hair clinging to their vulnerable young foreheads, but they seemed better all the next day, except weak. Then at night it was the same with Joanie.

The fourth day was like the rest, colder, with the same white storm outside, the children hunching silent upon themselves inside. Sometimes a small one sobbed a little in sickness and hunger, but it was no more than a soft moaning now, even when Lecia divided most of the little food that was left. The children, even Chuck, took it like animals, and then sat silent again, the deep-socketed eyes watching, some slyly gnawing at willow sticks and roots hidden in the palm.

Everybody around the fire was coughing and fevered now, it seemed to Lecia, the bickering going beyond childish things to quarrels about real or fancied animosities between their families. Once even Calla spoke angrily to Bill, defending her brothers.

" At least they aren't mama babies like you! "

" Mama babies! I wouldn't talk if everybody knew that my family got a start in cattle by stealing calves — "

" You can't say such things! " Calla cried, up and reaching for Bill, caught without his brace and unable to flee into the storm, Joanie crying: " Don't! Don't hit my brother! "

When Lecia returned, Chuck was holding the two apart, shaking them both. The teacher spoke in anger and impatience too now, and Bill's face flushed with embarrassment and shame, the sudden red like fever in his hunger-grayed cheeks.

Only Maggie with her poor feet was quiet, and Olive, sitting as though stunned or somewhere far away. The teacher knew that she should do something for this girl, only eight yet apparently so self-contained. Olive never spoke of her father now, as none of the boys teased Lecia about Baldy any more. Olive was as remote about him as everything else since the night she drank the milk, and found the ring on a twig.

Too weary to think about it, and knowing she must keep awake in the night, Lecia stretched out for a nap. When she awoke Olive was sitting exactly the same, but the places of Chuck and Eddie were empty — Eddie out in the blizzard after his night of sweating. When the boys returned with wood, weak, dragging, almost frozen, and with something that Lecia had to be told outside. There seemed only one willow clump left.

One clump? Then they must start digging at the frozen butts, or even pull down their shelter to keep the fire alive, for now the boys too were believing that the storm would blow forever. Yet toward evening there was a thinning above the smoke hole, the sun suddenly there like a thin disk of milky ice from the bottom of a cup. It was almost a promise, even though the storm swept the sun away in a few minutes and the wind shifted around to the south, whipping in past the block the boys had in the hole of the shelter. The children shivered, restless. Once Eddie rose from his sleep and fought to get out, go home. When he finally awakened, he lay down in a chill, very close to the fire, and would not move until a stench of burning cloth helped rouse him. Then he drank the bitter willow bark tea too and finally he slept.

Friday morning the sun came out again toward ten o'clock, the same cold, pale disk, with the snow still running along the earth, running higher than the shelter or Chuck, shutting out everything except the veiled sun. The boy came in, looked around the starved, listless circle at the fire, at the teacher too, with her face that had been so pretty Monday morning gaunt and sooty now.

He laid two red-tipped matches, half of all he had, in

the girl's lap. "I'm getting out," he said, and without a protest from anyone crawled through the hole and was gone.

The children were almost past noticing his desertion now, barely replying when spoken to. If the colds got worse or pneumonia struck, it would be over in a few hours. Maggie hadn't sat up since yesterday, lying flat, staring at the white storm blowing thin above the smoke hole. If any of them wondered how Lecia could keep the fire going alone, with nothing much except the willow butts left, none spoke of it. The teacher sat with her arms hanging between her knees, hopeless.

She finally stirred and put the matches away in waxed paper in her shirt pocket where her ring lay, buttoning the flap down carefully now. Joanie started to cough again, choking, turned red and then very white under the grime and grayness of her face, lying very still. Now Bill made the first gesture toward his small sister.

"Come here, Doll," he said gently, drawing her awkwardly from Lecia's lap, the child lifting her head slowly, holding herself away, looking up at him as a baby might at a stranger, to be weighed and considered. Then she snuggled against him and in a moment she was asleep.

After a long time there seemed a dull sound outside, and then Chuck was suddenly back, crawling in almost as though he had not left, panting in his weakness from the fight against the wind that had turned north again, and colder.

"Scared an eagle off a drift out there," he finally managed to say. "And there's a critter stuck in the snow — beyond the far willows. Small spring calf. Froze hard, but it's meat — "

Then the realization that Chuck was back struck the teacher. She was not alone with the children, and he too was safe for now. But there was something more. The boy who had resented them and his involvement in their plight — he had escaped and come back.

"Oh, Chuck!" the girl exclaimed. Then what he said reached her mind. "A calf? Maybe we could build a fire there so we can cut some off, if we can't get it all out." She reached for her boots. "But we'll have to go work at it one at a time — " looking around the firelit faces that were turned toward her as before, but the eyes alert, watching as though a morsel might be dropped, even thrown.

"I'll go with Chuck, Miss Lecia," Bill said softly. "He can show me and I'll show you. Save time hunting — "

The teacher looked at the crippled boy, already setting Joanie gently aside and reaching for his brace. She felt pride in him, and unfortunate doubt.

"He can probably make it," Chuck said, a little condescending. "It's not over an eighth of a mile, and I

found more willows farther along the way, the drifts
mostly frozen hard too. I blazed the willows beyond our
poles — "

"You'll be careful — mark everything," the girl
pleaded.

"We've got to. It's snowing again, and the sun's
gone."

It seemed hours since the boys went out and finally
the teacher had to go after them, appalled that the
younger ones had to be left alone, yet it must be done.
She moved very carefully, feeling her way in the new
storm, going sideways to it, from pole to pole. Then she
came to a place where the markers were gone, probably
blown down and buried by the turning wind. The boys
were out there, lost, in at least fifteen, perhaps twenty,
below zero. Without sticks to guide her way back, the
girl dared go no farther but she crouched there, bowed
before the wind, cupping her mouth with her mittens,
shouting her hopeless: " Boys! Chuck! O-hoo! " the wind
snatching it away. She kept calling until she was shaking
and frozen and then to a frightening warmth.

But now she had to keep on, for it seemed that she
heard something, a vague, smothered sound, and yet a
little like a reply. Tears freezing on her face she called
again and again until suddenly the boys were at her feet,
there before she could see them, so much like the snow,

like white dragging animals, one bowed, half carrying the other. For a few minutes they crouched together in desperate relief, the snow running over them as something immovable, like an old willow butt. Then, together, they pulled themselves up and started back. When they finally reached the shelter, out of breath and frozen, they said nothing of what had happened, nor spoke at all for a while. Yet all, even little Joanie, seemed to sense that the boys had almost been lost.

As soon as the teacher was warmed a little, she started out alone, not certain that she could make it against the storm, but knowing that she must try to get meat. She took Chuck's knife, some dry bark, waxed paper, the two matches in her shirt pocket, and a bundle of poles pulled from their shelter. Moving very carefully beyond the gap in the willow markers, she set new sticks deep, and tipped carefully with the new storm. She found the farther willow clumps with Chuck's blazing, and the brush pile the boys had made, and beside it the ice-covered head of the calf still reaching out of the snow. The hole they had dug around the red hindquarters, was drifted in loosely but easily dug out. Lecia set a fire pile there and felt for a match with her numb fingers, fishing in the depths of her pocket, something round in the way, her ring. But she got the match and lighted the fire under her shielding sheepskin coat. For a long time she crouched protectively over the flame, the wind carrying away the stench of burning calf hair. As the skin thawed, she hacked at it the way Indians must have done here a thousand years ago, their stone knives sharper and more expertly handled.

At a sound she looked over her shoulder and saw a coyote not three feet away, gaunt-bellied too, and apparently no more afraid than a hungry dog. But suddenly he caught the human smell, even against the wind, and was gone. He would have made a soft rug at the fire, Lecia thought, and wondered if he might not return to watch just beyond the wall of storm. But she was too busy to look. As the heat penetrated the meat, she cut off one slice after another until she had a little smoky pile, not much for nine people who had lived five days on one lunch apiece, but enough to bring tears that were not all from the storm. In this meat, perhaps three pounds, might lie the life of her pupils.

Lecia scattered the fresh ashes over the calf to keep the coyotes away and piled brush into the fire hole. Then she headed sideways into the storm, so violent that it was a good thing she had the strength of a little cautious meat inside her, for it seemed no one could face the wounding snow. Numb and frightened, she managed to hold herself, not get hurried, panicked, never move until the next broken willow, the next marker was located. So she got back, to find Chuck out near the shelter digging wood from the old clumps, watching, uneasy.

It was hard for the children to wait while the thinner slices of meat roasted around the sticks. When the smell filled the little shelter, Lecia passed out toasted bits to be chewed very slowly and well. It tasted fine and none asked for bread or salt — not even Olive, still silent and alone. She accepted the meat, but returned only distant gravity for the teacher's smile.

By now the white blizzard darkness was coming back, but before they slept there was a little piece of boiled veal for each and a little hot broth. It was a more cheerful sleeping time, even a confident one, although in the night they were struck by the diarrhea that Lecia had expected. But that was from the fresh meat and should not last.

By now Lecia could build a coal bed with rotten wood and ashes to hold a fire a long time, even with diamond willows, and so she dressed Maggie's feet, the girl light as a sack of bird bones, and prepared the night fire. For a while Chuck and Eddie kept each other awake with stories of coyote hunts and with plans for another morning of storm, the sixth. The two boys met the day with so much confidence that Lecia had to let them go out into the storm. Eddie, only ten, suddenly became a little old man in his seriousness as he explained their plans carefully. They would make a big brush pile so that they could settle out of the wind and work the fire until they got a whole hindquarter of the calf hacked off. So the teacher watched them go out very full of hope, the hope of meat, one of the half blankets along to drag their prize in over the snow, like great hunters returning.

Bill had looked sadly after the disappearing boot soles, but without complaint. He helped Lecia with the smaller children, washing at the grime of their faces that would never yield except to soap, and took them out into the storm and back while the teacher soaked Maggie's great swollen feet and tried to keep the girl from knowing that the bone ends of her toes could be seen in the suppurating pits of dying flesh. There were holes on the tops of the toes too, along the edges of her feet, and up the heels as high as the ankle. But above there the swelling seemed looser, the red streaks perhaps no farther up the bony legs. Once Bill looked over the teacher's shoulder and then anxiously into her face. Others had chilblains — his own feet were swollen from yesterday — but not like this.

" Will she lose — " he started to whisper, but he could not put the rest into words, not with a crippled foot himself.

The air was thick and white with new snow whipped by a northwest wind when Lecia went out for a little wood and to watch for the boys. But they were once more within touching distance before she could see them — very cold and backing awkwardly into the storm through the soft, new drifts, but dragging a whole hindquarter of the calf. It was a lot of meat, and surely the wind must finally blow itself out, the clouds be drained.

By the time Eddie and Chuck were warm they knew they had eaten too much roasted veal while they worked. Next Olive became sick, and Fritz, their deprived stomachs refusing the sudden meat, accepting only the broth. During the night the nausea struck Lecia too, and left her so weak that she could scarcely lift her head all the next day. That night Chuck lost his voice for a while, and Joanie was worse again, her mind full of terrors, the cough so deep, so exhausting that Bill made a little tent over her face with the skirt of his coat to carry steam from a bucket of boiling snow water to her face. Then sometime toward morning the wind turned and cut into the southeast corner of the shelter, crumbling the whole side inward.

The boys crawled out to patch it with brush and snow softened at the fire, Lecia helping dry off the children, as much as she could. Then when they were done and she laid her swimming head down, she heard a coyote's thin, high howl and realized that the wind was dying. Through the smoke hole she saw the running snow like pale windrows of cloud against the sky, and between them stars shining, far pale stars. As one or another awoke, she directed sleepy eyes to look up. Awed, Joanie looked a second time. " You mean they're really stars — ? "

"Yes, and maybe there will be sunshine in the morning."

Dawn came early that eighth day, but it seemed that nothing could be left alive in the cold whiteness of the earth that was only frozen scarves of snow flung deep and layered over themselves. The trailing drifts stretched down from the high ridge of hills in the north, so deep that they made a long, sliding slope of it far over the meadow and up the wind-whipped hills beyond, with not a dark spot anywhere to the horizon — not a yucca or fence post or willow above the snow. In the first touch of the sun the frozen snow sparkled in the deep silence following a long, long storm. Then out of the hills a lone grouse came cackling over the empty meadow, gleaming silver underneath as she flew, her voice carrying loud in the cold stillness.

But the meadow was not completely empty, for out of a little white mound of drifted willows a curl of smoke rose and spread thin and blue along the hill. There was another sound too, farther, steadier than the cackle of the grouse, a sound seeming to come from all around and even under the feet.

"A plane!" Chuck shouted hoarsely, bursting out into the blinding sunlight.

Several other dark figures crept out behind him into the frosty air, their breath a cloud about them as they stood looking northward. A big plane broke from the horizon over the hills, seeming high up, and then another, flying lower. Foolishly Chuck and Eddie started to shout. " Help! Hello! Help! " they cried, waving their arms as they ran toward the planes, as though to hasten their sight, their coming.

But almost at once the sky was empty, the planes circling and gone. For a long time the boys stared into the broad, cold sky, pale, with nothing in it except wind streaks that were stirring along the ground too, setting feather curls of snow to running.

" Quick! Let's make a big smudge! " Lecia called out, her voice loud in the unaccustomed quiet, and fearful. She threw water on the fire inside, driving smoke out of the hole while the boys set the snowy woodpile to burning.

Before the smoke could climb far, there were planes up over the north hills again, coming fast. Now even Fritz got out into the stinging cold — everybody except Joanie, held back by Lecia, and Olive, who did not move from her place. Maggie was lifted up by the teacher to watch through the smoke hole as something tumbled from the higher plane, came falling down. Then it opened out like the waxy white bloom of the yucca, and settled toward the snow, with several other smaller chutes, bright as poppies, opening behind.

There was shouting and talk outside the shelter and while Lecia was hurrying to get the children into their caps and boots, a man came crawling into the shelter with a bag — a doctor. In the light of the fire and a flashlight he looked swiftly at Joanie and then at Olive, considered her unchanging face, lifted the lids of her eyes, smiled, and got no response. Then he examined the poor feet of Maggie, the girl like a skin-bound skeleton in this first sharp light, her eyes dark and fearful on the man's face.

The doctor nodded reassuringly to Lecia, and smiled down at Maggie.

"You're a tough little girl!" he said. "Tough as the barbed wire you have out in this country. But you're lucky somebody thought to try snow against the gangrene—" He filled a little syringe and fingered cotton as he looked around to divert the child.

"All nine of you alive, the boys say. Amazing! Somebody got word to a telephone during the night, but we had no hope for any of you. Small children lost eight days without food, with fifty inches of snow at thirty-eight below zero. Probably a hundred people dead through the country. The radio in the plane picked up a report that six were found frozen in a car stalled on the highway — not over five miles from town. I don't see how you managed here."

The doctor rubbed the punctured place in the child's arm a little, covered it, smiling into her fearful eyes, as men with a stretcher broke into the front of the shelter.

When they got outside, the air was loud with engine roar, several planes flying around overhead, two with skis already up toward the shelter and a helicopter, hovering like a brownish dragonfly, settling. Men in uniform were running toward the children, motioning where they should be brought.

They came along the snow trail broken by the stretcher men, but walking through it as through the storm. Lecia, suddenly trembling, shaking, her feet unsteady on the frozen snow, was still in the lead, the others behind her, and Chuck once more at the end. Bill, limping awkwardly, carried little Joanie, who clung very close to her brother. They were followed by Calla and Eddie, with Fritz between them, and then the stretcher with Maggie. Only Olive of all the children walked alone, just ahead of Chuck, and brushing aside all help.

There were men running toward the bedraggled, sooty little string now, men with cameras and others, among them some who cried, joyous as children, and who must be noticed, must be acknowledged soon — Olive's father and Dale Stever of the yellow plane —

But for now, for this little journey back from the smoke-holed shelter of snow, the awkward queue stayed together.